She had to find hi drastic...

A few days before Christmas Christine plucked up her courage and walked into the garden. The path to the front door was shoveled clean. At least she wouldn't leave any footprints. She tried the door handle. Locked, of course. She lifted the doormat. No key. At home a spare key was hidden in the garage. Here Jim only had a small shed for his tools. She walked over to it only to find a padlock on its door.

She let out a big sigh. Was there a back door? She had never looked before. She crept around the side of the house. Yes, there was a door but would also be locked. Windows? All closed.

Back at the side of the house a drop of water trickled down her face. She looked up. An icicle was melting and dripping. Another thing caught her attention. A small loose board hung at an angle and under it—something metallic. Christine stretched up and lifted the board. A key! She had found the key. The house key or the one to the shed?

Quickly she took it off the hook and crept back to the front door. She looked around. It had gotten dark in the meantime. She didn't see anybody on the street. The key fit and turned with a crunching sound. As much as she wanted to go inside, Christine knew she had to get home. Maybe tomorrow. She locked the door again and hung the key back up under the loose board. She couldn't help but smile, one step closer. She felt like skipping all the way home. Now the search could begin. She couldn't talk to anyone about it, of course, not even Ellie. She had gone to her grandmother's for Christmas. Christine wasn't sure whether she would be able to wait until after the holidays. As things turned out, she had to.

The year is 1958 in Peachland, Okanagan BC. Twelve-year-old Christine meets a man renovating an old house in her neighborhood and immediately feels a bond between them. Even though her mother reacts strangely after hearing the man's name, Christine visits Jim often after school and learns a lot about flowers and gardening. She is heartbroken when he suddenly leaves without a good bye and is determined to find out where he is and why he left. As she unravels the mystery, dark secrets are revealed that make her uncertain if Jim will even want to come back.

KUDOS for *The Old House*

I found the book hard to put down and was as curious about who Jim was as Christine. I thoroughly enjoyed the book. I found the wholesome goodness mixed in with this little girl's daring plans to find out who Jim really was—and where he suddenly disappeared to—to be very interesting. It kept me turning pages. I normally get bored easily with books. I tend to put then aside and then read on later, but I actually read this book in two days because it was so hard to put down. I kept formulating ideas in my mind as to who Jim would really turn out to be. All in all, a very enjoyable book. – Taylor, reviewer

The Old House by Gisela Woldenga is classified as a young adult, although I would probably classify it as an adolescent, since it seems to be geared more toward middle school and early high school than late high school and beyond. Still, it is a heart-warming and very moving story of a young girl's quest...*The Old House* is short and can be read in an afternoon. At least I did it that way. I quite enjoyed it. And while I am not sure I would call it a page-turner, it certainly was an engaging read. – *Regan, reviewer*

THE OLD HOUSE

Gisela Woldenga

A Black Opal Books publication

GENRE: ADOLESCENT/DRAMA

This is a work of fiction. Names, places, characters and incidents are either the product of the author's imagination or are used fictitiously, and any resemblance to any actual persons, living or dead, businesses, organizations, events or locales is entirely coincidental. All trademarks, service marks, registered trademarks, and registered service marks are the property of their respective owners and are used herein for identification purposes only. The publisher does not have any control over or assume any responsibility for author or third-party websites or their contents.

THE OLD HOUSE
Copyright © 2012 by Gisela Woldenga
Cover Design by Jackson Cover Designs
All cover art copyright © 2012
All Rights Reserved
PRINT ISBN: 978-1-937329-75-4

First Publication: DECEMBER 2012

All rights reserved under the International and Pan-American Copyright Conventions. No part of this book may be reproduced or transmitted in any form or by any means, electronic or mechanical, including photocopying, recording, or by any information storage and retrieval system, without permission in writing from the publisher.

WARNING: The unauthorized reproduction or distribution of this copyrighted work is illegal. Criminal copyright infringement, including infringement without monetary gain, is investigated by the FBI and is punishable by up to 5 years in federal prison and a fine of $250,000.

ABOUT THE PRINT VERSION: If you purchased a print version of this book without a cover, you should be aware that the book is stolen property. It was reported as "unsold and destroyed" to the publisher, and neither the author nor the publisher has received any payment for this "stripped book."

IF YOU FIND AN EBOOK OR PRINT VERSION OF THIS BOOK BEING SOLD OR SHARED ILLEGALLY, PLEASE REPORT IT TO: lpn@blackopalbooks.com

Published by Black Opal Books **http://www.blackopalbooks.com**

I would like to acknowledge my faithful writer's club in Port Moody, BC.

CHAPTER 1

1958:

"Mom, someone is moving into the old house on Vicary Road!" Twelve-year-old Christine bounded up the stairs of the porch and into the kitchen. "I saw a moving van and people carrying stuff inside."

"Oh, good." Her mother turned around. "About time someone took care of it."

"It better be a handyman," her father said. He had come up from the cellar carrying a bunch of carrots. "It needs a lot of doing, the house, the garden."

The old house at the end of Vicary Road had been empty for many years. Christine had never seen anyone living there. Other kids in her neighborhood thought it was haunted and avoided the place. Now the garden was overgrown and the trees stuck out their branches, wild and crooked. At night they looked like scrawny arms.

She nodded. "Yeah, I wonder who the people are."

After school the next day, Christine couldn't curb her curiosity. She went to the house and stood by the sagging fence. She couldn't see anyone. Were there kids, a mother and father? Why weren't they playing outside? Christine pushed against the rusty gate and took a few steps into the garden. Then she saw the door open. A man stepped out. He waved to her.

"Hello there! Want to come have a look?"

Christine rubbed her nose and hesitated. Mother had always warned her. "Don't go with strange people." But this man had a big smile and was rather handsome, though, of course, old. If she didn't go too close it should be safe. She decided to find out who he was and walked along the path towards him. He put out his hand.

"My name is James, Jimmy to some. The Jimmiest guy you can find." He laughed.

Christine stayed back a bit. "I'm Christine. I live down the street. How come you moved here?"

"Well, someone has to look after this place. It has been standing empty for too long and it's in a bit of a mess now, but I'll put it back into shape." He swept his arm through the air. "All this will take a while. Come by any time, okay?"

Christine nodded. "Okay. See you." She waved and went on her way home. He's all by himself, she thought, nobody to help him. Maybe Dad can on weekends. He's a

THE OLD HOUSE

handyman. She skipped up the steps to her house. "Mom, I met the new man in the old house!"

Her mother's voice came from the living room. "You did? You were nosy again." She appeared in the kitchen and threw a hand full of wilted flowers into the trashcan. "Didn't I tell you to be careful with strangers?"

"Don't worry, I was, but he's all by himself and he is very friendly. His name is James—or Jimmy." Christine laughed. "He said he was the Jimmiest guy in the world."

Her mother turned around suddenly with a startled look on her face. "Jimmiest guy, he said?"

"Yeah, isn't that funny?" Christine wondered why her mom was so surprised and why her eyes had gotten so big.

As her mother busied herself at the sink, Christine kept on. "Maybe Dad can help him with the house some time, because Jim has no one else."

Her mother stopped for a moment. "I don't think so. People want to do their own thing, have their own ideas. Besides, he could get help if he wanted to. There are plenty of men in town who want to earn extra money."

"Maybe he is too poor for that. I can ask Dad," Christine persisted. Mother didn't answer. "I have a project for school. I better start on it." Christine ambled down the hall into her room. Why had her mother acted so funny when she heard the man's name? Tomorrow she would do some investigating and try to find out his last name and where he came from.

School took longer than usual the next day. Christine's class had to present a play at the end of the school year. Miss Web, her teacher, had written it herself and wanted to select the students for the different roles. Christine had hoped to get the leading part, but teacher decided she needed a smaller girl for it. So Christine ended up with the role of the mother.

"Not to worry," Miss Web consoled her. "You have lots of lines to learn. It's an important part."

Christine sighed. "All right. As long as it's important."

Inwardly she grumbled. *Why not Helen? She's bigger than me, much better as a mother.* But Helen couldn't memorize very well. She always had trouble reciting poems. Christine grabbed the pages of the play and started on her way home.

Now to find out more about Jim.

When she arrived at the old house her eyes popped. What had happened here? The wobbly fence and rusty gate had disappeared and she saw a large heap of new wood and planks on the ground. She also noticed big bald patches where high weeds had been. Wow, she thought, Jim had been busy. And there he was, already waving at her.

"Want to help?" he called.

"How did you do all this?" She scrambled over some old fence posts.

THE OLD HOUSE

"Well, the day has twenty-four hours and I sleep for six of them, so I had lots of time. Want an orange?" He pointed to a bottle of Orange Crush.

"Yeah, sure, thanks." Could she ask him? Mother would say she was too forward. But how else could she find out? "Where do you come from and why come here?"

Jim took a moment. "Last stop was in Toronto. Construction and landscaping. But it gets too cold in the winter, only good for snow shoveling. I like it better here in the Okanagan. The weather is nice and in the winter I can work inside the house. It needs a lot of repairs."

Next step. "What's your last name?"

Jim laughed. "What's yours?"

"Willard, Christine Willard."

Jim took a drink out of his bottle and then he smiled at her. "Okay, fair enough. It's Hansen, James Hansen. But don't tell anyone else." He winked at her.

"You want to stay incognito?" Christine was proud to use the new word she had just learned today. "Is someone after you?"

Jim shook his head and chuckled. "Don't worry, I didn't escape from anyone. I just need to work alone for a while at something useful."

Christine got up. "I better get home. Mom will be waiting. See you tomorrow?"

He got up and grabbed his tool bag. "Right on. Careful climbing over the wood."

On her way home Christine wondered: *Can I tell Mom and Dad the man's name? He asked me not to.* But Mom and

Dad weren't strangers, they were her parents. They probably didn't care anyway. She was about to run up the porch steps when the door opened. Dr. Merrit? What was he doing here? He smiled at Christine.

"Hi Christine. How are you?"

"Fine." She got worried. "Why are you here?"

"Your father had a bit of a spell. He's resting now, he'll be all right. Your mom will tell you all about it." He patted her shoulder. "Stay healthy, okay?"

Christine watched him striding down the street. She had known Dr. Merrit forever. He would come when she had the flu or the measles. Mom went to him because of her headaches. How come Dad was sick? She opened the door and called. "Mom? Where are you? What's wrong?"

Her mother closed the bedroom door softly behind her. "Shh! Dad's sleeping. He will be fine. He came home and felt very weak. Dr. Merrit said his heart was slow." She shrugged. "Whatever that means. He wrote out some prescription."

Christine didn't know what to think. "In school we learned that the heart has to beat regularly or else—"

"Dr. Merrit told me we have pills now to help. So don't worry. I'm going now and get them from the drugstore. Go do your homework. I'll be right back." Mother grabbed her purse and disappeared down the steps.

Christine stood for a moment. She rubbed her nose. Dad would get better, the medicine would help. But how sick was he really? She crept down the hall and opened the bedroom door as quietly as she could. Her dad was sleeping

THE OLD HOUSE

but he looked pale. She had never seen him like this. Whenever he took a nap on the couch his cheeks were rosy. She stood for a while staring down at his still face. "Get better soon," she whispered, then tiptoed out of the room and closed the door. *Tomorrow I'm going to ask the teacher what a* slow heart *means.*

CHAPTER 2

During the next two days Christine didn't get a chance to visit the old house. At school rehearsals had started on the play and she wanted to memorize her part as quickly as possible. She found it annoying during rehearsals to have to look at the pages all the time. And then her father was home. Dr. Merrit thought it would be better for him not to go to work and rest for a few days. Christine was still worried about him. His color had come back but he slept a lot. He never used to do that. At recess she went to Miss Web.

"Do you know what it means to have a slow heart? The doctor said that's why my dad doesn't feel well."

"Oh dear. I'm not sure, but it sounds like his heart is weak. Maybe your doctor can explain it better. Does he take medicine?"

Christine nodded. "I have a doctor's book at home. I'll look it up. Maybe it will explain it. Thanks." I should have known, she thought. Teachers only knew about English, math and geography.

At home Mother asked her to weed the vegetable patch. "I don't want your dad to do that right now," she said.

Christine sighed and grumbled. "Can I get more allowance for doing that?"

"Do I get more money for washing, cooking, and tending to your dad?" Mother asked back. "You have to pitch in when it's necessary."

So Christine spent a whole afternoon trying to separate weeds from small peas, beans, and lettuce plants. In the end she found the variety of weeds quite interesting. She stopped to think. The old house must have millions of them in the garden. The man had so much more work to do than to weed just a vegetable patch. And he had already done so much in a short time. At supper Christine asked, "Can I check up on Jim tomorrow at the old house? I'm curious how much more work he has done. He told me his last name. It's Hansen, James Hansen."

Something clattered to the floor. "Oh sorry." Her mother bent down and picked up her fork. She got up to get another one. But she rummaged around in the drawer for a long time.

"You okay?" Father asked.

THE OLD HOUSE

"Yes, yes, just clumsy." But Mother was strangely quiet for the rest of the evening and seemed to be far away with her thoughts.

Since the next day was Saturday, breakfast was later and relaxed. Christine took her time eating her pancakes and bacon slices. Today she was going to check up on Jim and the old house, no matter what. He probably has the whole new fence up by now, she thought. After Dad had gone into the garden, her mother turned to her.

"I don't want you to go see Mr. Hansen so often," she said.

Christine stood still. "Why not? I just want to check up on his work."

Her mother looked at her. "You're so trusting. You don't know him. He could be anybody."

Christine knew what was coming. "He's not a bad man. I know all about being careful. He's friendly and he works hard." *I'm going even if you don't want me to.*

Her mother sat down. "Why do you like him so much?"

"Because..." Christine fumbled for the right words. Then she shrugged. "Because he's...different, he's funny and serious and—and honest. He told me his name and that he worked in Toronto before."

Her mother sighed and looked down at her hands. "All right. But don't stay too long. We have lots to do here with Dad not feeling well. And don't ever go into his house, you hear?"

"Don't worry, I won't." *Yippee, I can go!* "Mom, if you would come and meet him you could find out what he's like."

Mother gave her a long look, then shook her head, and turned away. "Better not," she said.

What does "better not" mean? Strange.

After she helped with the breakfast dishes, she dashed out the door and down to the end of the street and the old house. Just as she had expected, a good part of the new fence was up. She also noticed more bald patches amongst the weeds. But Jim wasn't outside. Was he still eating breakfast? Tools were piled by the door. Christine wandered up to the trees. A few gnarly branches had been cut off and stacked up on the ground. But where was Jim? She could knock on the door—maybe not a good idea. Just when disappointment crept into her stomach, she heard motor noises. An old truck chugged up the lane and stopped.

There was Jim. Christine let out a sigh of relief. He jumped down out of the truck and slammed the door shut.

"Hey!" he called. "It's been a while. Look what I bought."

"Where did you buy this truck?" It was so old.

Jim patted the hood. "Looks well used but it will do. See what else is in here."

The back of the truck was full of boxes and containers with plants. Jim pointed to each of them. "These are dahlias and marigolds. Here are some rhododendrons, red and

THE OLD HOUSE 13

white. And these are lilies, different kinds. Just for good smells I'll plant some lavender too. I even bought a hanging basket for the trellis over there." He rubbed his hands together as if he couldn't wait to get started.

Christine had never seen so many flowers in one heap. "Where do you want to plant them all?"

Jim started to unload the truck. "Oh, I have places in mind as soon as I get rid of the rest of the weeds. Some plants need shade and some more sun. I want the garden to be colorful."

"I can help," Christine offered.

He handed her a few smaller boxes. "Put them in the shade under the trees." Then he looked at her. "Why aren't you playing with your friends? It's Saturday."

"Maybe later. They play the same things all the time. I like this better." Christine needed to convince Jim that helping him was important to her.

Jim shook his head. "But this is work and you might get dirty. I don't want you to get in trouble with your parents."

"That's okay. Mom said I could, but not for too long. Just for a while." She grabbed another container and added it to the ones already under the trees. She stood and looked at them. The garden at home had lots of plants and flowers, too. They had been there forever and would appear every spring and summer. From then on they only needed watering. This was like creating something brand-new.

Jim had unloaded everything and fastened the hanging basket on the trellis by the entrance door. "Looks more like someone is living here," he said. "Now you run along. You've been a great help."

Christine would have liked to stay much longer, but she knew Mother was waiting. "See you tomorrow," she called and walked out of the newly installed gate. That garden was going to be the best in the neighborhood, she thought.

Halfway home Ellie, her school friend, drove up beside her on a bike. "Hey, wanna come bike riding?"

"Have to ask my mom."

Ellie jumped off the bike and pushed it alongside Christine. "What were you doing at the old house?"

Christine was glad Ellie asked. She just had to share her enthusiasm with someone. "I helped the man in the garden. He just moved in. You should've seen all the flowers he bought. I didn't believe it!"

Ellie frowned. "Why would you help him? That's the man's job, and he is old. I saw him."

"No, he isn't. He has a bit of grey hair, so what. He's really nice and interesting."

"Okay," Ellie conceded. "But ask your mom. We could ride down along the lake."

Christine skipped up the porch steps. "Mom, can I go bike riding with Ellie?"

Her mother was stirring batter in a big bowl. The usual Sunday cake.

THE OLD HOUSE

"Then you have to do your chores in the afternoon. It's up to you," Mother answered.

"Okay, let's go." Christine retrieved her bike out of the garden shed and followed Ellie down the street towards the lake.

The subject of Jim and the old house didn't come up again during their ride. Ellie talked a lot about the school play and Christine told her about her father's sickness. Only on their way home Christine had an idea.

"Ellie, why don't you come with me next time and meet Jim. You'll be surprised how much work he's done."

Ellie thought for a moment. "Okay, but don't expect me to work in the garden. I'll just go and look."

"Great! If you come Mom won't be so worried about me going there." *Brilliant solution.*

⋐⋑⋐⋑

When they went to the old house after school the next day, Jim was happy to meet Ellie.

"I wondered if you had any friends at all," he said to Christine. "A person has to have friends, it's important. Life can be lonely without at least one."

Christine and Ellie looked at the new flowerbeds and Ellie was duly impressed. On their way home she said, "He looks better close up, not quite so old."

Christine giggled. "Told you so." Maybe Ellie was one of the friends Jim had talked about, she thought.

CHAPTER 3

During the next weeks Christine barely had time to think about Jim and his garden. At school, rehearsals for the play were going on three times a week. The end of the school year was near which also meant report cards. The only subject that bothered Christine was math. She did what she could, but for some reason the explanations the teacher gave didn't stick in her mind for very long. Most days on her way home she just walked by the old house and waved to Jim when she saw him working in the garden.

Her father had gone back to work, but he was tired when he came home in the evening and had to sleep for a while before supper. Very unusual. He didn't talk much about how he felt. Whenever Christine asked him he'd only said, "Better," and patted her head.

So she couldn't believe her ears when he said one Saturday morning, "How about you and me going over to

Jim's and take a look at his garden? I would like to meet him."

Christine hopped from one foot to the other. "Oh, Dad, that would be sooo wonderful. Why doesn't Mom come too?"

"You can ask."

But Mom shook her head. "You go on, I have work to do," she said and walked out of the room.

Jim was chopping wood when they arrived. He stopped and waved.

"This is my dad. He wants to meet you," Christine called as she opened the gate. She noticed the whole fence was up and more flowerbeds had been created. Everything looked so clean and orderly. Jim wiped his hands on his shirt and shook her father's hand.

"I'm happy to meet you," he said. "You have a very busy daughter, and I think she's pretty smart, too." He winked at Christine.

She giggled. "Maybe. I didn't get my report card yet."

"Would you like to look at the house?" Jim asked her father. "I've concentrated on the garden first, so the inside is still rough. That's my next project."

Dad nodded and Jim opened the front door. Her mom had told her not to go into the house, Christine remembered, but Dad was going, so it was okay. While the men talked about plumbing and repairing, she wandered around the rooms. The floors creaked and crackled and she spotted a few loose boards. But it was clean. There were no

THE OLD HOUSE

spider webs like in other old houses. The windows were a bit dirty. If Mom were here she would wrinkle her brow and clean them right now. The hallway was short and narrow. A door stood half-open. Christine peeked inside. Jim's bedroom. Just a bed, a dresser and a chair. What a small house. But cute for one person, almost like a big playhouse.

Dad and Jim were still talking. Christine went out into the garden. She couldn't even see any weeds any more. Then she smelled something sweet. She wrinkled her nose. She remembered Jim telling her about the lavender. There it was. *Maybe I should plant some in our garden. Mom would love it.*

Just when she heard her father say, "We better get home now," Christine had an idea. She trotted over to Jim.

"We are performing a play at school in two weeks. Would you like to come and see it? I'm in it."

"Is it a funny play or a drama? Are you the lead character?" Jim's eyes twinkled. Christine noticed it and giggled again.

"Nooo. But I'm the mother and it's an important part. We have two performances, Friday and Saturday evenings. Please, come."

Jim rubbed his chin. "I'll certainly try." Then he looked at her father. "What else is your daughter into?"

Dad laughed. "I wish I had her energy." They shook hands.

"Come any time and inspect," Jim said.

On their way home Christine couldn't wait to ask. "Did you like Jim?"

Her father nodded. "He's an all right guy. Knows what he's doing. I wonder if he has a family."

"You mean parents or a wife?" Christine also had thought it strange that nobody ever came by to visit him.

Dad shrugged. "Well, it's his business. I'm glad he's doing such a good job with the house and garden. I still wonder what brought him here."

Christine already knew the next question she was going to ask Jim.

That opportunity came two days later. On her way home from school she saw Jim sitting under a tree, reading. This was the first time she hadn't seen him working. She called, "Can I come over?"

"Sure," he answered.

She saw a wicker chair and table. That was new. She pointed to them. "They're nice for company." Then she turned to Jim. "What are you reading?"

He put some papers aside. "Oh, just some newspapers and letters." But he had a frown on his face and seemed to be unusually serious.

Christine hesitated. Could she ask him or was that again too nosy? But she really wanted to know. "Are the letters from your family?"

"One is from my sister, the other just business." Jim folded them and stuffed them into the envelopes. "Why do you want to know?"

THE OLD HOUSE   21

Now Christine felt a bit embarrassed. "I just—wanted to know if you have family. Nobody ever visits you. I'm glad you have a sister."

Jim had a far-away look in his eyes. He sighed. "Yeah, the only one left. My parents died long ago." Then he smiled. "But now I have you as a friend. And I'm going to see your play."

Christine's heart jumped. "Oh, goodie! What day? My parents are going Saturday. Why don't you come too? Then you can meet my mother."

Jim looked up at her. "No, it's better I go Friday. That way you have a good audience both days." He got up. "I'll show you something."

Christine followed him to the side of the house. Her eyes widened. There were figures made of stone: a girl holding a bowl, a boy pumping water into a bucket, a huge frog and another boy with a fishing rod and a fish dangling on it. "Oooh," was all she could say.

Jim lifted the boy statue and carried it into one of the flowerbeds. "I'll hide them around the garden to surprise people."

Christine got excited. "That is so neat! Now I know what I'll get Mom for her birthday: a girl like the one over there."

"Okay, I'll find one for you," Jim said.

Christine knew she was late coming home again. At least she knew now that Jim had a sister. She was going to tell her parents about the garden figures. The front door was locked. She knocked and called. No answer. Where was Mom? She never went shopping in the afternoon. Christine retrieved the spare key from the shed and opened the door. She called, "Mom? Where are you?" Again nobody answered. Then she spotted a piece of paper propped up on the table. She read, *Dad is sick again. I am at the hospital. Please, go to Mrs. Burns next door.* It was signed, *Mom.*

Christine's enthusiasm collapsed. Dad must have gotten sick again at work. What was wrong with him? He was okay yesterday. Would he ever get better? She didn't feel like going over to the neighbor's. She would have rather gone back to Jim's. But she didn't want to worry her mother any more than necessary. With a sigh she dropped her schoolbag in the corner. She really should do her math, but right now she didn't feel like it. She wouldn't be able to concentrate on numbers. She closed the door behind her and walked over to the house next door.

Mrs. Burns was an elderly lady who used to babysit Christine once in a while. She had a dog and a cat, and Christine always marveled at how well they got along with each other.

"They grew up together," Mrs. Burns had explained, "just like brother and sister."

Today she had a frown on her face. "I do hope your father gets better." She took the cookie jar from the shelf. "As long as they know what they're doing at the hospital. Sit down and have some cookies. Tell me about school."

THE OLD HOUSE

Christine was actually glad to have someone to talk to. It took the edge off the worry about her father. Mrs. Burns listened, nodded, and even promised to attend the school play.

Then Christine asked, "Have you seen the old house? It sure has changed."

"I'll say. Who is living there now? He must be some worker."

"I'm a good friend of his. He'll show you around if you go by."

Mrs. Burns waved her hand. "He has better things to do than trotting through his garden with an old lady." She looked out the window. "Here is your mother now. Let's find out about your dad." She opened the door. "Come in and have some tea."

Christine thought her mother looked tired as she walked slowly up the steps. Mrs. Burns touched Mom's shoulder.

"Come sit down and have a rest. Tell us what's going on." She went to the stove and put on a kettle.

"Is Dad all right?" Christine asked.

Mother took a deep breath. "Yes, for now. They want to try a different medicine, a bit more powerful, they told me. But—" She stopped. A tear ran down her cheek. "He looked so weak and pale, I don't know..."

Christine's insides trembled. "He isn't going to die, is he?"

Mrs. Burns put cups and saucers on the table and poured the tea. "Let's keep our hopes up and say a prayer."

"If his health doesn't improve, he might not be able to work anymore. That will be hard for us," Mother continued. "We have the house and some savings but I might have to get a job—somewhere. I'm not sure what I could do." Her hand trembled when she lifted the tea cup.

"I'll help," Christine chimed it. "Carry out newspapers, babysit—"

Mother smiled. "Let's just wait and see. Finish your school year. You're not even thirteen yet."

After a few days father was allowed to come home. He seemed to feel better. Now Mother and Christine could breathe a bit easier. Christine tried to put thoughts about what would happen if her father died way into the back of her mind. Young people didn't die, did they? She considered her father young, not like Mrs. Burns. Christine also hoped he would be well enough to see the school performance.

CHAPTER 4

On the morning of the show, the back stage of the small theatre was all noise and chaos. Costumes and props lay everywhere and needed to be gathered up and put into their rightful places. Some parents were helping out, and one father had to secure parts of the scenery again because one over-eager boy had knocked down a paper-mache tree.

Christine was excited. Mom had helped her to get one of her own old dresses shortened and had added an apron. She wound Christine's long dark hair around her hand and put it into a bun. And for the first time in her life she put on lipstick and even rouge on her cheeks. Christine felt so grown-up, just like a real mother.

That night she peeked through the curtain. Had Jim come? She hadn't talked to him for a few days. She couldn't see him in the audience. "Please, don't forget," she mumbled.

After all the chaos beforehand, the performance went well. None of the kids got stuck on their lines. The audience applauded, and Christine saw Jim waving to her. Perfect, she thought. Now she was crossing her fingers that Dad would also be able to come tomorrow.

As it turned out Dad was feeling well enough. He even bought a red rose for Christine. "You did a great job," he told her. "It looks like you'll be a good mother someday."

Christine thought that life couldn't get any better, especially now that school was out for two months. As she had promised, she had made up her mind to deliver the daily newspaper every morning even though some of the dogs in the neighborhood scared her. They would bark and jump at her bike, and she had to be quick to get away. She also had to get up earlier in the morning than she liked but she wanted to have some pocket money. Ellie was forever nagging her to go to the ice cream parlor. She always seemed to have more money than Christine. Maybe her parents were rich. But Christine decided to save some of her pay, just in case Dad wasn't able to work anymore. For now she was happy to go swimming in the lake, visit Jim, and go bike riding with Ellie. Even clearing out weeds in the yard wasn't such a big thing anymore. Looking at the work Jim had done made her job seem rather insignificant.

THE OLD HOUSE 27

If only Dad wouldn't get sick again. One day she had talked to Jim about it. He had told her about an invention that had been tried out.

"It's a small box with wires and a battery. The wires have to be connected to the heart, so they can help it to beat properly. The box is worn outside."

Christine couldn't even imagine putting wires into anyone's heart. That would certainly kill a person. She shuddered. "I don't want Dad cut open. He would die right there."

Jim patted her shoulder. "Not to worry. This device is only in the beginning stages. They call it a Pacemaker. But the scientists have to work more on it before they use it on more people."

When Christine told Ellie about it she laughed. "That's gross. I think Jim told you a big story. I bet he made it up."

"No, Jim never tells lies," Christine argued. "He must have read it somewhere in a magazine. He reads a lot, you know."

"Uh huh," was all Ellie said.

છ૭છ૭

The summer went by too quickly. Jim had bought a garden figure for Christine to give to her mother on her birthday and he kept it hidden in his yard. The girl stood on a pedestal and held a bowl with flowers in her hands. It also had long hair like Christine. The day before the birthday

Christine took it home, wrapped red ribbons around it and put a bunch of lavender out of Jim's garden into the girl's bowl. Jim had hidden a small card amongst the flowers with big letters *Happy Birthday*. Christine knew she somehow needed to find out what he had written.

As Christine hoped her mother liked the little stone girl. She said it was the best birthday present ever and placed it between two rose bushes. Father had known about the present and had even made sure that her birthday cake was topped with a figure of the same girl, all made out of icing sugar.

Christine saw Mom picking up Jim's card but she put it quickly into the pocket of her apron without reading it. Christine was dying to find out what Jim had written and devised a plan. When Mom and Dad were talking and having tea in the living room that evening Christine sidled up to the apron hanging by the towels, fished the card out of the pocket and took it into the bathroom.

She opened it carefully and read: *Happy birthday and many more happy years. Jim.* That was all? Oh, well it was nice of him to write at all, Christine thought. When she wanted to put the card back into the apron she saw just in time that Mom was in the kitchen for some more tea. *Oops, better be careful and wait.* Christine retreated into her bedroom. Only after Mom and Dad were sitting down again she tiptoed back and slipped the card back into the apron pocket.

ℰℐℰℐ

THE OLD HOUSE

Although Jim was still working on the house, he was gone quite often. Sometimes a few days, once even a whole week. He never told Christine about it. Sometimes she got worried but she didn't dare ask him where he went. Dad said it wasn't her business. She was just happy when he appeared again. She couldn't imagine the old house without him or a day without at least seeing him there.

When school started, it took a while to get settled with a new teacher and a few new kids in the class. So Christine didn't notice right away that Jim had gone again. "He'll come back soon," she told Ellie. "It's probably business."

But weeks went by without a sign of him. One afternoon Christine saw a man working among the flowers. She leaned over the fence.

"Hi, why are you working here?"

The man looked up and Christine recognized Mr. Whiting, a neighbor from a few houses down the street.

"I'm taking care of the house and garden," he answered. "Jim is gone for a while."

"Gone? For how long?" Christine's throat tightened. "He never said anything about it."

"Probably didn't want to say goodbye. Not to worry. I'll take good care of all this." Mr. Whiting grabbed the rake and went back to work.

Christine stood still. Her stomach had a big lump in it. Didn't want to say goodbye? But he was her friend, the best one she'd ever had. Something was wrong. A friend wouldn't leave like that. By the time she arrived home tears were running down her face, she couldn't hold back loud sobs.

"What's wrong, Christine? What happened?" Mother wrapped her arms around her. "Are you hurt?"

"No—yes," Christine gasped. "Jim is gone and didn't even say goodbye. Something is wrong, Mom!"

Mother stroked her hair. "But he went away before and came back."

Christine shook her head. "Mr. Whiting is taking care of the house now. He was working there. He said—he said—"

"Oh, hush, child. There has to be a reason." Mother took a breath. "There's always a reason."

Christine couldn't think of one. "He could have told me."

"Sometimes people can't talk about it," Mom said.

"But he is my friend. He said so."

Christine tried to calm down. Maybe Jim would write? Did he go back to Toronto? But why? He liked it better here and he had the house. He wouldn't leave it all, would he? And he had said that she was his friend, had come to the school performance. Did he run away from someone? She had to tell Ellie.

"Weird," Ellie said. "I told you he was. Could be he escaped from somewhere and got found out."

THE OLD HOUSE

"No way, he's not a criminal. You read too many Nancy Drew books. He's a good man." Christine started to cry again.

"Okay, okay. We just have to find out why he left."

"How? I don't know where he went—unless—maybe he told Mr. Whiting?"

Now there was an idea. He did get mail before. If it was an important letter, Mr. Whiting would have to send it on, wouldn't he? Then he had to have an address.

"Come on, we'll ask Mr. Whiting about it." Christine was already pedaling off on her bike. Both girls went up to the house and knocked on the door.

Mr. Whiting looked surprised. "Christine, you again? What now?"

Christine's heart was thumping. "It's very important that I know where Jim went, I have to write him."

Mr. Whiting scratched his chin. "Can't tell you. I promised him I wouldn't tell anyone, and a promise is a promise, right?"

"But—but it's very important."

"Yeah," Ellie chimed in. "A matter of life and death."

Mr. Whiting laughed. "Now, now, girls. Who knows, Jim might come back some day. Sorry, you'll have to wait."

Christine's heart sank. There goes my idea, she thought. Why couldn't Jim have told her? Like Mother had said, there had to be a reason. What possible reason could there be? Would she ever find out?

CHAPTER 5

With school getting harder and Christine having more homework than before, she tried not to think too much about Jim. But she missed his big smile and the chats they used to have. In the back of her mind she knew she had to find out why he had left and where he was.

Snow started to fall in November and the old house and garden looked like they were asleep under a blanket. The statues of the boy and girl wore jackets and hoods of snow. Christine hoped that Jim might come back for Christmas. But as it got nearer to the school's Christmas concert there was still no sign of him. Ellie figured he would probably stay with his sister. After all who wants to be alone at Christmas?

Christine's ears perked up. "I wonder where his sister lives. He got a letter from her before. Maybe..." She rubbed her nose. Another idea formed in her head. "Know what?

Maybe the letter is still in the old house. We'll have to find it. But how to get into the house?"

"Well, we can only go when Mr. Whiting isn't there," Ellie said.

"We don't have a key. And there is no window open in the winter. Breaking in is a crime. I don't want to end up in prison. Can you imagine what my parents would say? But I'll find out anyway at what times Mr. Whiting is in the house. I'll watch every day."

Christine felt a surge of energy. At last she could do something instead of waiting. She would see smoke coming out of the chimney when she went to school in the morning, so Mr. Whiting had to be in the house. By lunchtime it had stopped and by the end of the school day all was quiet.

A few days before Christmas Christine plucked up her courage and walked into the garden. The path to the front door was shoveled clean. At least she wouldn't leave any footprints. She tried the door handle. Locked, of course. She lifted the doormat. No key. At home a spare key was hidden in the garage. Here Jim only had a small shed for his tools. She walked over to it only to find a padlock on its door.

She let out a big sigh. Was there a back door? She had never looked before. She crept around the side of the house. Yes, there was a door but would also be locked. Windows? All closed.

THE OLD HOUSE   35

Back at the side of the house a drop of water trickled down her face. She looked up. An icicle was melting and dripping. Another thing caught her attention. A small loose board hung at an angle and under it—something metallic. Christine stretched up and lifted the board. A key! She had found the key. The house key or the one to the shed?

Quickly she took it off the hook and crept back to the front door. She looked around. It had gotten dark in the meantime. She didn't see anybody on the street. The key fit and turned with a crunching sound. As much as she wanted to go inside, Christine knew she had to get home. Maybe tomorrow. She locked the door again and hung the key back up under the loose board. She couldn't help but smile, one step closer. She felt like skipping all the way home. Now the search could begin. She couldn't talk to anyone about it, of course, not even Ellie. She had gone to her grandmother's for Christmas. Christine wasn't sure whether she would be able to wait until after the holidays. As things turned out, she had to.

❧❧❧

The holidays were just too busy to search the old house. With last-minute Christmas shopping, buying a tree and decorating it, and helping with baking and cooking Christine wouldn't have been able to get away. Also, her dad wasn't always feeling too well, again.

But Christmas morning was wonderful: Christine's big present was a pair of roller skates. She had clamored for them for so long. Finally there they were, bright and shiny. Since snow covered everything outside, the only place she could try them out was on the cement floor in the basement. Not much space but enough to practice her balance.

Neighbors got together on Boxing Day for Christmas cheer. A lot of kids took their new sleds out to zoom down the hills nearby, and Christine just had to take part in all the yelling and whooping.

Two days before New Year's, in the middle of the night, Christine heard her mother call, "Christine, wake up. You have to help me. Dad is sick again."

Christine rubbed her eyes. What a time to get sick. Mother came into her bedroom, looking scared.

"Quickly, get dressed. Run to Dr. Merrit's house and wake him up. He has to come right away".

Christine didn't take time to change, just put pants and a jacket on over her pajamas, boots on her bare feet and ran. It took a while after she rang the bell and knocked on Dr. Merrit's door a few times before he came out. Together they walked quickly back to her house. As Christine waited, huddled on a kitchen chair, she had a bad feeling. To get sick during the night felt three times as bad as during the day. She remembered from her own colds, when she couldn't stop coughing.

THE OLD HOUSE

Finally Dr. Merrit came out of the bedroom. He looked at Christine with sad eyes.

"You have to be strong, Christine, you and your mother. Your dad couldn't fight any more. His heart just stopped."

Christine sat still. Dad died? Gone? Forever?

"If you want you can come and join your mom. Your dad looks very peaceful."

Christine got up from the chair. She couldn't think. Something heavy and dark filled up her head. Her stomach had a lump in it. She followed Dr. Merrit into the bedroom. He put his arm around her shoulders as she stood and looked at the still figure in the bed. Was he really dead? He seemed to be asleep. Her mother sat on a chair and held her father's hands. She looked up at Christine. Her face was wet with tears.

"Mom, is he really dead?" Christine whispered.

Her mother nodded, let go of her father's hands, and pulled Christine close to her. "We are alone now. We have to go on without him."

"I'll leave you," Dr. Merrit said. "I'll notify the funeral home. I'm so very sorry I couldn't do anything more for him."

The darkness in Christine's head finally gave way and she started to sob. Mother got up. They held onto each other. After a while Mother said, "Let's go into the kitchen. Dad is resting now, no more pain."

Christine took one more look back. Really dead?

All through the rest of the day, she repeated the words to herself: *No more pain for Dad.* Mother went over to Mrs. Burns who had a telephone and was going to notify the neighbors of her father's death. It didn't take long and the front door was opening and closing every few minutes with people coming and going. That activity dulled the pain in Christine's stomach and gave her the feeling that they were not totally alone.

Only after her father's body was taken away did it hit her that he would never come home again. He would never pat her head, joke, and laugh again. She tried hard to stop crying so much because she wanted to be strong and help her mother. But Mother said, "We both will cry a lot and often. That's okay."

The day of the funeral, the house was almost too small for all the people visiting. Many of them brought cakes and casseroles, flowers and lots of cards with gold writing and fancy envelopes. The pastor said in his sermon, "Let us celebrate your father's life, not his death." Except that Dad couldn't celebrate with them, Christine thought.

Ellie and her parents came too and it was good to talk to her again. Christine couldn't tell her that she had found the key to the old house. *I'll do that later. I feel too sad right now.*

THE OLD HOUSE

When school started again Christine tried hard to concentrate on her studies. She knew her dad would have wanted that. He always used to say that she was smart and she should work hard so she could make something of herself. Now that he was gone she would have to find a good job after she finished school. Maybe work in a garden shop? That would be fun.

At home everything had quieted down. Once in a while when she came home from school she found her mother's eyes full of tears. Mom went more often to Mrs. Burn's house for tea and a chat. Often, at night, Christine couldn't help her own tears from dropping on her pillowcase. At least Mother wouldn't see it. She missed her dad a lot.

After a few weeks went by Christine decided that it was about the time to focus on Jim's house. She had lost her father. She wanted to get her friend Jim back. Ellie jumped up and down when she told her about finding the key. "Christine, you're a genius. Let's get to work."

They met at the house after dark. Christine took the key off the hook and opened the front door. Ellie hesitated. "I'll stay outside as a look-out. The house inside is too creepy for me."

"Fine."

Christine had taken a flashlight along. She didn't dare switch on the lamps. Anyone outside could see the light. But how could she find anything with just a thin beam of light? First she went into the small living room. A desk stood against the window. Some papers lay on top. She shone the flashlight on it. No letter, no envelope. She tried the drawer. *Oh good, it's not locked.* Carefully she took some of the papers and spread them on the desktop. She didn't want to be nosy. All she needed to find was the letter of Jim's sister. She heard Ellie's voice.

"Someone coming down the street." Then, "It's okay, they just went the other way."

"Please, God, let no one come into the yard," Christine mumbled. She tried not to feel defeated yet. But she couldn't find any letters. She arranged the papers the way they had been, closed the drawer and tiptoed into the kitchen.

Again she heard Ellie's voice. "Hurry up, I'm freezing to death."

Christine didn't answer. The contents of the kitchen drawers showed only cooking utensils. She shone the light around the walls. Near the door she spotted a leather pouch hanging from a nail. Something white was sticking out. Could it be? She pulled at it: three envelopes. One of them was hand-written. She opened the letter. It read: *Dear Jim. It's all right to come and stay for a while.* Christine didn't bother to read the rest. She knew this had to be his sister's writing. The envelope had her address on it. She stuffed it into her pocket and put the letter back into the pouch. She had found it! Now she knew where Jim lived.

"I'm coming out. All clear?" she called.

"Yeah, hurry up."

THE OLD HOUSE   41

Christine switched the flashlight off and locked the door. "I found it, Ellie, I found the address." In her excitement she nearly slipped on an icy patch. She hung the key back up and both of them scooted out of the yard and onto the street.

"What are you going to do now?" Ellie asked.

"Write a letter to this address and ask Jim to come back, that we miss him. I'm also going to tell him that my dad died."

Ellie was doubtful. "I don't think he cares about that.

"Well, Jim has met him and liked him and maybe— anyway, that's what I'm going to do."

When Christine sat alone in her room trying to write the letter, she wondered, would Jim be mad at her for breaking into his house? After all, how else could she have found his sister's address? Besides he had left without telling her and without explaining why. That wasn't nice for a friend to do. Quite simply, she had the right to find out.

She found a piece of lined paper and started. Her plan was to write it first in rough draft and then carefully onto a piece of her mother's fancy letter paper. Slowly the words came. *Dear Jim. How are you? I am very sad that you left and did not tell me. Please, come back soon. We miss you. My dad died and now I need you as a friend. Your friend forever, Christine.*

She read it over a few times and thought it was okay. Now for a nice piece of paper to transfer it to. She had to make sure her mother wasn't close by. But she found her ironing in the backroom.

Christine slipped into the living room to her mother's desk. She had to be quick before Mother came back. Her desk drawer held lots of letter paper and envelopes. They were decorated with small flowers, different ones on each page. Christine selected one of her favorites: purple pansies. Back in her room, she made sure not to misspell any words and used her best handwriting as she copied her letter. After she had folded it and stuffed it into the envelope, she sat back. Jim would have to answer her. What if he didn't? Then Christine would simply write again. His sister had to know where he was. She was the only family he had. He wouldn't just disappear.

She hid the letter in her school bag. Tomorrow she would go to the post office and buy a stamp. And then she would have to wait.

CHAPTER 6

Christine's birthday at the end of January came closer, and she couldn't imagine how to celebrate without her father. He had been the one with special birthday cakes and surprises. Maybe it was better to forget about it. But Mother said that it was necessary to have a party.

"Thirteen is an important age. From now on you are more grown-up. Why not invite Ellie and maybe a few other girls? Dad would have liked that."

Mother was probably right. To wait for her next birthday a year from now was just too far away.

On the birthday morning two parcels lay on the breakfast table.

"Can I open them now?" Christine asked. Mom nodded. Despite Christine's misgivings about this day she got excited. She unwrapped the first one: a pair of boots. "No more sore toes," she giggled. Now the second one.

She unfurled a blue sweater, the one she had seen in the shop window. She jumped up and hugged her mother. It was going to be a good birthday.

After school, Ellie and two other girls joined Christine at home. They also brought presents: a book, a bell for her bike, and some fancy hairpins. The birthday cake had a big *thirteen* on it with pink roses all around. After they each ate a big piece, they had fun playing games. Time went by so fast that the girls were sorry to go home again for supper.

That night in bed, Christine remembered her last birthday when her dad was still alive. Maybe he was listening somewhere?

"I had a great birthday," she said. "It would have been perfect if you had been here. I miss you. Don't go too far away. Love you." And with the warm feeling that he had understood, she fell asleep.

❧❧

The next afternoon on her way home from school Christine went by the old house.

Everything looks so dead without Jim, she thought. Will he ever write me back? The answer she was waiting for came in a different form than she had expected. Mother looked puzzled when she handed her an envelope with Christine's address on it.

"Whom were you writing to? This is the first letter you ever got. Did you get a pen pal?"

THE OLD HOUSE

45

Christine's heart started pounding. Her fingers shook as she ripped the envelope open.

She read, *Dear Christine. Thank you for your letter. Jim is not living here anymore but I will pass your note on to him. Best wishes, Alice.*

Christine burst into tears.

"What's going on?" Mother took the letter from her. "What is this? Christine, what are you up to?" Her face looked stern and her voice was scarily quiet.

Christine could only answer between sobs. "Dad died and—Jim went away—without telling me why and where—and I—want him to come back. He lived with his sister and now he's gone again."

"How did you get this lady's address?"

Christine knew she had to tell the truth. She could only hope that her mother would understand. She told her about looking for the key, searching the house, and finding the letter. Mother listened without interrupting. She got up from the chair and stood by the window for a long time. Christine got anxious. Finally, her mother turned around.

"I don't want you to search any longer for Jim. He must have had a good reason to leave. Peoples' lives are...sometimes difficult. It's up to him to come back or not."

Christine didn't understand. "Then why did he come here and rebuild the old house and garden? He said he liked it here. Why would he leave it all? And he said I was his friend."

Mother looked at her. "Let it rest, Christine. Just promise me not to bother his sister again. I don't want you to intrude into their lives."

Christine couldn't say anything. What did Mom have against Jim? He was just a friend, someone to talk to. Christine knew she couldn't let it rest.

During the next few days, she wracked her brain for what else she could do to find Jim. She told Ellie about the letter from his sister.

"At least she wrote back and he'll get your letter. Maybe he'll answer now," she said. "Was your mom mad at you?"

Christine nodded. "Yeah, we had a long discussion. And then she said, 'Let it rest'. Well, I won't."

Ellie looked at her. "Are you in love with Jim?"

Christine stopped in mid-step. "No, of course not, don't be stupid! He is as old as my dad. If I fall in love it'll be with a guy a bit older but not that much. Jeeze, what were you thinking?" She had to laugh. "It's just that I can talk to him about anything. He's so smart." He had already taught her so much about flowers and planning a garden.

"Okay, I was only wondering. I'll keep my fingers crossed for you." At least Ellie was supportive.

A few weeks went by. The snow had melted but the gardens still looked soggy and sad. Here and there under the trees, snowdrops poked out their white heads. It would still be a while until the bushes and trees would sprout their first leaves. Christine had kept up her nightly conversations

THE OLD HOUSE

with her dad. No, he couldn't answer but talking to him made her disappointments lighter. Jim hadn't written yet.

A few days later, at suppertime, her mother said, "I'll be working a few days a week, so you have to do some house work."

"Oh, wow! Where did you get the job?"

"The post office. I'll be sorting mail." Her mother didn't seem to be too excited about it.

"You said you wanted to work. I'll help if you tell me what to do."

"But some days it will be late in the evening. You'll be by yourself." Mom looked at bit worried.

"I'll be okay, I'm thirteen now, remember? More grown-up?"

Mother gave her a sideways smile. "Yes, I know, and getting smarter every day. But I'll have to be sure you're responsible and dependable. And keeping up with your school work."

"Don't worry so much, Mom." *I'm not a baby anymore.*

When Christine came home from school the next day, her mother had gone to work. She'd left a note with things to do: peel potatoes and put them on to boil, set the table, put the dishes away. Nothing to it, thought Christine. She also wanted to find the envelope from Jim's sister that Mother had put away. Ellie had come up with an idea.

"Why not find out if his sister has a telephone?" she'd suggested.

"But she lives in Vancouver. All I have is her address and I don't have a phone," Christine said

"So what? The post office has."

Christine grunted. "Yeah, my mother works there, remember?"

"Not all the time. If you have Alice's address you can phone the operator and find her number."

Christine hesitated. "But that costs money. Okay, I have some from my paper route. If it works I can talk to Alice, if she even lets me. She might be sick of me snooping."

Ellie was sure. "She just has to listen."

Christine located the envelope in her mother's desk. She only needed to find out which day her mother was working during the evening so she would be home in the morning and afternoon. That time came two days later. After school Christine and Ellie went straight to the post office. The postmaster showed them a booth with a phone.

"You have to pay me once you're done," he reminded them.

"Okay, we will," Christine promised. Her fingers trembled as she dialed *zero*. She had to swallow and tried to keep her voice steady as she told the operator the name and address of Jim's sister. Ellie stood by with both fingers on both hands crossed. Then—yes, Alice had a phone! Christine jotted the number down on the envelope and took a deep breath. That was the first step.

"Well? Phone her right now," Ellie said.

THE OLD HOUSE

Christine shook her head. "I'll have to think about it. I don't know yet what to say. Maybe tomorrow." She didn't want Ellie around either. This was too personal.

At home she wrote down what she wanted to ask Alice: where was Jim? Was he okay? Was he coming back? But what was Christine going to say if Alice told her—like Mother would—"It's none of your business"? Then she would apologize and hang up. The end. Maybe what she was doing was all wrong. She sighed. Her stomach hurt. *Okay, this is the last thing I'm going to try.* After that? She didn't know.

CHAPTER 7

When Christine's mother was working evenings at the post office, Christine picked up her courage and went after school to make that phone call to Jim's sister. Her heart pounded; it made her ears ring. I have to do this, she told herself, I have to sound confidant, and I'm not going to babble. As before the postmaster showed her a phone booth. Once in there she took a deep breath. Again her fingers trembled as she carefully dialed the numbers, counting them out loud. She heard the phone ring, then Alice's voice, "Hello?"

Christine had to swallow again. "Hello, this is Christine. I wrote you a letter. Thank you for writing back."

"Yes, Christine. I'm so sorry that your father died. Are you and your mother all right?"

Alice's tone gave Christine hope. "Yeah, we're okay. But I have to know how Jim is and when he's coming back. It's really important."

There was a pause. Then, "I have talked to Jim. He told me to tell you that he'll be back in the spring. He was in the hospital for a while but he's better now."

"In the hospital? Why? Is he okay? He's coming back?" *Now I'm babbling!* She heard Alice laugh.

"Yes, he wants to see the spring flowers in his garden. Nice to hear from you. Take care of yourself. Bye, Christine."

"Thank you so much! Bye." Christine heard a click, Alice had hung up. Christine replaced the receiver and stood still. Jim was coming back. He was really coming back. That was all that mattered. Hospital? Did he have a slow heart, too? Was he going to die like Dad?

Christine shook her head. It had to be something different. That was another thing she had to find out. Then it hit her. Alice had been nice. She hadn't been cross with her. Christine could have jumped around with joy. But she had to keep all this a secret from her mother. She had told her not to bother Alice again, and Christine had disobeyed. But everything was going to be okay. Now she didn't mind waiting another month.

Ellie was a little disgruntled when Christine told her about the phone call. "Why didn't you tell me? I would've been there cheering you on."

THE OLD HOUSE

53

"No, Ellie. I had to do that by myself. But it was your idea about getting the phone number. Thanks for that. And Alice was really nice. I was a bit scared."

Ellie seemed appeased. "Well, you owe me one. How about helping me with that crazy essay we have to do?"

Christine was too happy to object. "Sure, come by tonight. We'll do it together."

"Why didn't you ask what was wrong with Jim?"

Christine shook her head. "A long-distance call costs money, you know. I didn't want to stretch it out. Besides, that might have been too personal."

With the knowledge of Jim's return, everything looked brighter, even grey days with rain showers and occasional snowflakes. Christine's mother worked four times a week, two of them in the morning and two later at night. Since Christine had more to do around the house to help with cleaning and cooking, the thoughts about her father's death had faded into the background.

The churning pain of his loss had turned more into a soft sadness. Quite often Christine would remember his laugh and the things he used to say to tease her. Some nights she still talked to him before going to sleep, especially when her day had been eventful. She wanted him to know about the recent phone call to Alice, and Jim coming back. Also that she had enrolled in some after school drama classes and art classes. He had always encouraged her to learn how to paint.

One afternoon after school, Christine found her mother sitting at the kitchen table.

"Hi, Mom. Guess what? Teacher gave us the choice of what painting to do: still life, landscape, whatever, even a person. But I can't do that. I think I'll try a still life."

Mother looked at her. "That will have to wait. Sit down. I need to talk to you."

Christine's heart sank. There was Mother's quiet, edgy voice again. What had she done? She had done all her jobs, did her school work, got a good grade in her last essay—what? She sat down.

"Mr. Miller, the postmaster, tells me that you made phone calls, one all the way to Vancouver. Is that true?" Mother kept looking at Christine.

Oh no! Christine's throat started to close up. *That traitor!* She bit her lip. No use denying it. "Yes, I did."

"Whom did you call?"

"Alice. Mom, I—"

"Even after I told you to leave those people alone, not to bother them again?"

Christine just nodded.

Her mother got up. "Why? Why can't you let it be? I have enough to cope with, your father dead, me working, and you not doing what you're told."

Tears started to roll down Christine's face. "I had to, Mom. I needed to find out if Jim was okay. Alice was really nice. She wasn't cross with me. And Jim is coming back soon. He was in the hospital." *Mom might as well know.*

THE OLD HOUSE   55

"Hospital?" Her mother turned away. After a few minutes she asked, "How did you pay for the phone calls?"

"I still had some money from my paper route."

"Okay, at least you did that right." Her mother turned back. "Well, what's done is done. But please, no more secrets. It's only you and me. We have to trust each other, okay?"

"Yes, Mom. I'm sorry." Christine couldn't help feeling that there was something her mother wasn't telling her—her shocked look when she heard Jim's name, always telling Christine not to go and see him, and now being so angry because she had phoned Alice. Maybe grown-ups were allowed to have secrets and kids weren't. Right now Christine was just glad that Mother had calmed down and was putting on the vegetables for supper.

✍✍✍

By the end of February, the sun shone more often and crocuses filled the gardens in all colors like Easter eggs. The first green spikes of daffodils even poked out of the flowerbeds. Christine was checking the old house every day on her way home from school. So far she only saw Mr. Whiting doing some clean-up work outside. She told herself to be patient, that Jim would keep his promise and come very soon. But she had never been good at waiting. It was one of the hardest things for her to do. Her mother hadn't mentioned the phone calls again, and Christine was sure she would eventually change her mind about Jim once she had met him.

ഏഏ

One day, in the first week of March, on her way home from buying some sugar, Christine saw smoke coming out of the chimney of the old house. It was close to suppertime. She stopped in her tracks. Could it be? Was Jim finally back? Christine stood by the fence. Light shone through the windows. Yes, it had to be Jim. Mr. Whiting never stayed that late. I'll check again tomorrow, she thought. I want to be very sure before I'll tell anyone.

That night Christine had a hard time falling asleep. There were so many questions she wanted to ask Jim. And she had to confess that she had broken into his house. Again she imagined her father being with her.

"If you can help, please, Dad, don't let Jim be mad at me. You understand that I had to do the things I did, right? I wish you were here." With a big sigh, she pulled the comforter up to her neck and, with her fingers crossed, finally fell asleep.

CHAPTER 8

On her way to school the next morning Christine again saw smoke coming out of the chimney of the old house. Yes! It had to be Jim. How much time did she have to investigate? I'll be as quick as I can, she thought. As she walked through the garden the front door opened. Jim smiled at her. Christine stopped.

"It's okay, I'm back." He looked a little thinner than before.

"I'm...I'm so glad," was all Christine was able to say.

"Come by after school. I have something to give you. Then we'll talk. You better not be late for school." He waved and closed the door.

The rest of the way to school Christine's mind switched from happiness at Jim's return to worry about what he wanted to talk about. But he had smiled. Maybe there was hope that he wasn't too angry with her. She was the last one in class to slip into her seat.

The teacher gave her a puzzled look. "Is everything all right?"

"Yes, sorry." Since Christine's father died the teacher had been a bit more lenient with her, asking quite often how her mother was doing. Christine looked over to Ellie, who raised her eyebrows. Christine gave her a thumbs-up sign. Ellie would know what that meant.

At recess, Christine couldn't wait to tell her. "Jim is back. He stood in the door and waved at me. I'm just a bit worried."

"Why?" Ellie raised her eyebrows again. "That's all you wanted, for him to come back."

Christine rubbed her nose. "Yeah, but he wants to talk to me, maybe give me a lesson about not snooping. And he has something for me, too. I hope he isn't too mad at me."

"Oh, heck, you worry too much. Want me to come along?"

Christine shook her head. "Don't think so. I'll tell you all about it later, okay?"

"Okay, but don't you tell him about me being there when you broke into the house. It'll spoil my reputation."

Christine couldn't help laughing. "Your reputation? What's that about?"

"Well, don't you know? My mom always says, a good reputation starts very early in life. I don't want to lose mine already."

THE OLD HOUSE   59

Christine was still giggling. "Now who's worried? I won't tell." She had never associated *reputation* with the things kids did. That was something adults had to worry about, at least according to books she had read.

When the bell rang at the end of the school day, Christine was the first one out the door. She jogged down the street to the old house. Her heart pounded. She hesitated, and then knocked on the door. Jim answered right away.

"Come in, Christine." He looked at her. "I think you have grown." He held the door open. Again Christine hesitated. "It's okay. I would think your mother cautioned you about going into a strange man's house. But scout's honor, I'm only Jim. I don't want you to freeze out here. Besides, we already know each other so well."

Christine felt better. After all, she had been in the house before with her dad. The living room was warm and cozy with glowing logs in the fireplace.

"Sit down," Jim said. "We'll have to get re-acquainted. Sorry, I made you worry about me. And I'm even more sorry about your dad dying."

I have to tell him. "I felt sad that you left without saying good bye. I thought you were my friend. That's why…" She didn't know what else to say.

Jim nodded. "Strange, isn't it? Because I'm you friend I left the way I did."

Christine was puzzled but she kept quiet.

"I'm just curious," Jim continued. "How did you get my sister's address?"

Well, here I go, even if he kicks me out. Christine started slowly, trying to find the right words. Then it spurted all out: thinking of the envelope, finding the key, getting into the house and taking the envelope. After that writing the letter and later making the phone calls. She stopped, quite out of breath.

Jim chuckled. "You are one determined little lady. I'm flattered. Did your mom find out?"

Since Jim had laughed she felt hopeful. "Yeah, she did and gave me heck. So, you're not terribly angry with me? I mean, I broke into your house. I could end up in jail."

"After all this time?" He got serious. "There are reasons why I left so suddenly. I didn't know if I would be able to come back. Alice told you that I had to go to the hospital. But all is well for now." He got up and retrieved a letter from the desk. "I want you to give this to your mother. Make sure she opens it. Don't let her throw it away."

Christine was puzzled. "Why would she do that?"

"Oh, there could be reasons. I'm counting on you. It's very important."

Again, Christine thought that Jim was talking in riddles. She would have to find out about the mystery eventually. "I'm so glad you're back," she said.

Jim smiled. "So am I. See you soon."

THE OLD HOUSE

Once outside again Christine felt like dancing down the street. Jim wasn't angry, he was back for good. All was well. Now she had to hurry to get home. Mother was working and it was Christine's job to look after supper. Why did Jim write a letter? she wondered. Why doesn't he just come over and talk to Mother? Grown-ups are so funny sometimes.

Mother's reaction to Jim's letter was even stranger. Her face turned pink. She weighed the letter in her hand, put it on the table, and then picked it up again.

"Aren't you going to open it?" Christine asked.

"Maybe later. Did he…say anything about what you did?" Mother was still looking at the letter in her hand.

Christine nodded. "Yeah, but he laughed. He wasn't cross with me."

She filled the sink with soapy water. It was her turn to clean the milk bottles for the next morning's pick-up and wash and dry the rest of the dishes. Mother took the letter, went into her bedroom, and closed her door. She could have read it here, Christine thought. Why was she so secretive? After a long time she was tempted to knock at her mother's bedroom door. Was she okay?

When she finally appeared again, Christine noticed that her eyes were red. Mother had been crying.

Why would Jim make her cry? "Mom, what's wrong? Are you okay?"

"Yes, don't worry." Mom's voice was still a bit shaky. She wiped her eyes and smiled a little. "We have to sit down and talk, not today but soon."

Christine knew not to ask any more questions. But something in the letter made her mother cry and smile at the same time. Would the upcoming talk finally explain her mother's strange reactions to Jim's name and her reluctance for Christine to visit him? And now this letter. Grown-ups sure made life difficult.

CHAPTER 9

The next day was Saturday, so Mother didn't have to go to work. At breakfast, Christine couldn't wait any longer.

"Mom, what did Jim write? Why did you cry?"

Her mother held the coffee mug in both hands and slowly swirled the coffee around. "It's a long story and some of it will upset you. But maybe you're old enough now to understand."

"Does it have a happy ending?"

Mother got up and poured more coffee into her mug. She added some milk, and then sat down again. "Part of it is happy. But you might as well learn that sometimes life twists and turns before it straightens out. Let's get the house in order and then we'll talk." She walked to the sink and looked out the window into the garden.

Christine had an uneasy feeling. To her way of thinking the household chores could have waited. Was Mother nervous about their talk? She had sounded so serious. But Christine's curiosity made her clean up her bedroom faster than usual. However; Mom took her time with the rest of the housework. When Christine found her finally sitting on the sofa in the living room, she let out a sigh of relief. Mom patted the seat beside her.

"Sit down." She put an arm around Christine's shoulder. "This is difficult for me, so remember, Dad and I love you more than anything, even if he's not here anymore."

Christine's throat tightened. "Mom, is this really terrible?"

"No, just...a strange twist of life. Please, listen, okay? I'll tell you a story of a young girl. She was nineteen years old when she met a handsome soldier. It was nineteen forty-five, almost the end of World War II. The soldier was on leave but had to go back. They fell in love and promised each other to meet again after the war. When the war ended the girl waited. His letters had stopped coming and the soldier didn't return. She found out that he had been badly wounded but she didn't get any messages from him. After a while she thought he had died." Her mother took a breath. A few tears trickled down her face. Then she continued. "The girl found out that she was pregnant."

Christine gasped. "She was having a baby?"

THE OLD HOUSE

Mother smiled a little. "Yes, but to have a baby and not be married was shameful, so the girl had to leave her work and move away. Her father had died in the war, and her mother was so upset with her that she was of no help. The girl found a place here in the Okanagan and gave birth to a baby girl. When the baby was two years old, the girl met a man who fell in love with her and married her. From then on he treated the baby like his own." Mother stopped again.

"What was the baby's name?"

"Her name is Christine."

Christine sat still. "That's my name. Am I—are you that young girl?" *No way!*

Her mother nodded. "Yes, and I still thank God that your dad came along and married…us."

Christine's thoughts whirled around like leaves in the wind. *Unthinkable, it couldn't be.* "So, I was two when Dad came. But then he can't be my real father?"

"Your dad brought you up, cared for you, and loved you. In my book that's a real father, just not your biological father."

"Was it—the soldier who didn't come back?"

Her mother had a far-away look in her eyes. "Yes, he never even knew he had a daughter."

"Didn't you want to know if he ever came back? Maybe he didn't die. Why didn't you try and find out?"

"What good would that have done? If he had lived, he might have his own family. His wife wouldn't have liked the idea of another child showing up. Besides, I was married to your dad. He wouldn't have appreciated me searching for your real father."

Suddenly Christine started to cry. She couldn't help it. "I can't even think of Dad not being my—Dad. He's the only one I know."

Her mother put her arms around her. She had tears in her eyes too. "I knew you would be upset. He loved you as much as if you were his own child. Never forget that. He's probably still watching over you. If he hadn't died, I wouldn't have told you any of this."

Christine tried to stop her tears. "But what has Jim's letter got to do with this? Did he know the soldier?"

"No. Do you remember that I got upset at Jim's name? That I didn't want you to spend so much time with him? Dad was still alive and I didn't want any problems in the family. There was a reason. Jim is the soldier."

Christine stared at her mother. "Jim is my father? My real father?" *Couldn't be!* She started to rock back and forth. Her mind whirled. *Dad is not my dad, Jim is my real dad. One dad died and the other is alive.* She leaned her head against her mother's chest and looked up at her. "Are you at least real?"

Her mother stroked Christine's head. "I'm the only mother you have."

They sat quietly together for a while. Christine tried to say something but her mind didn't know where to begin.

THE OLD HOUSE

"I know, this is a lot for you to swallow," Mother said. "The one reason that Jim went away was that he didn't want to interfere in our family life. The other one was that he needed another surgery, related to injuries from the war. I just don't know how he found us in the first place."

Christine straightened up. "Didn't he write that in the letter?"

"No, I guess he'll have to tell us, won't he? You have to promise me that you don't say a word to anyone about this, not even your best friend."

Christine just nodded. Of course she couldn't talk to Ellie about it. What would she say about the fact that Christine had two fathers? And that Mom hadn't been married when Christine was born? There was really nobody she could talk to about it.

The rest of the day she tried to make sense out of all she had found out. She had liked Jim right from the start. Did he already know when they met that she was his daughter? Did he find out later? If she hadn't written Alice that her dad had died, he might have never come back. Christine was glad she had persisted, even if she had made Mother mad and broke into Jim's house. But she couldn't go back to the old house right now.

What would she say? "Hi, Dad"?

Impossible. Things were different now, a tiny bit awkward. Although she was relieved that the soldier had been Jim, not anyone else, she just needed some time to let it all sink in.

She also needed to know the rest of the story. How did he find out where Mom and Dad lived or that he had a daughter? Again, she would have to ask him, plain and simple.

"Mom, why don't you invite Jim over for tea or something? Then he can tell us all about it," Christine suggested after supper.

Mother shook her head. "What would the neighbors think? Your father isn't even gone for a year and me inviting a single man to dinner?"

"But everybody knows Jim by now. They wouldn't care."

Mother was adamant. "I'll write him a letter back. You can bring it to him."

"You have to meet him, Mom. I'm sure he's waiting for that."

Mother got angry. "Christine, leave this to the grown-ups. This isn't like a romantic novel."

But it was, kind of, Christine thought. That night, in bed, she had a long talk with her dad. As far as she was concerned, he was still her father with all the memories of her thirteen years attached to him. Would he give her a hint as to what she could do? But she could almost hear him say, "It's none of your business."

CHAPTER 10

Mother looked tired the next morning. After breakfast she handed Christine a letter. "Take it to Jim and let him read it," she said. "It will explain a lot of things and he'll understand."

"Did you write this during the night?" Christine asked.

"Yes, I didn't get much sleep." Mother poured herself another cup of coffee. "Let him read it in peace, don't bother him."

"Can I go to Ellie's after?" Christine needed to go somewhere and talk to someone else.

"Okay, as long as you don't tell her our secret."

"Oh no. I would never do that." Christine took the letter and wandered down the steps. She had butterflies in her stomach. She wasn't sure at what to say to Jim. Everything felt different now. Yes, he was still her friend. That wouldn't change. It was how it all started. *Maybe he doesn't know yet that I know that he's my real father.* He would have to read the letter first.

When Jim opened the door, all Christine's fears faded and the butterflies flew away. He smiled. The house smelled like fried bacon, and on the table sat a plate with two sunny-side-up eggs.

"Good morning, you're early. Aren't you sleeping in on Sundays? I used to, sometimes till noon."

Christine couldn't help but giggle. "Mom would kick me out of bed."

"So, she's strict, is she? Want an egg? Join me. I hate eating alone." Jim slid the bacon pieces onto another plate.

"I just had breakfast, but—okay." Christine couldn't say no, it just felt good to be here. She watched him break the egg into the frying pan. *My father? That's so weird.*

"Here you are. Want some bacon?"

While they ate Jim asked, "School okay? Any more plays?"

Christine shook her head. "Nope, too busy with math, English essays, and science."

"Hmm, that's a load." Jim sat back. "Did your mom read my letter?"

"Yes." Christine pulled the envelope out of her pocket. "She wrote you back. She cried when she read your letter."

Jim looked at the letter in his hand. "I'm sorry. I didn't want to make her cry."

THE OLD HOUSE

Then he looked at Christine. "I'll read this and, if you want, come by later again, okay? If you can't, come tomorrow. We'll talk for a bit."

"I'll go to my friend Ellie for a while. Then I'll be back. Thanks for breakfast."

Outside Christine wondered, *Will he tell me everything about himself and how he found us?*

As it turned out Ellie and her family weren't home. Somehow that was all right. Christine couldn't talk to her about what was on her mind anyway. Would she ever be able to tell Ellie? Christine wouldn't break her promise to Mother not to. It was going to be so difficult to keep it all a secret. She didn't feel like going home. Instead she walked down to the lake and sat on a bench. So many thoughts were churning around in her head. Mom didn't want to see Jim because of the neighbors, and Jim would probably respect her wishes. Why would the neighbors care? To them, Jim was just the man in the old house. So, when would they finally meet? Christine didn't want Jim to leave again. She gave a big sigh. Why do grown-ups make everything so complicated? Finally she got up again. Almost lunch time, Mom would be waiting.

Her mother had the table already set when Christine walked in. "Well, did you deliver the letter?"

"Yes, and he made me breakfast."

Mother smiled. "Maybe you shouldn't eat any lunch? Oh well, you're still growing."

"Jim wants me to come back. He said, we should talk."

Mother was quiet for a while. Then she said, "Since you're his daughter and our go-between-person, you might as well."

Christine bit into her sandwich. "Why don't you meet Jim in a park or something, you know, when other people are at work? That's pretty safe. Nobody would see you."

Her mother laughed. Christine hadn't heard her laugh for so long, it startled her. "What's so funny, Mom?"

"You are." Mother took out her handkerchief and wiped her eyes. "Always thinking of ways to bring us together. I'm just glad you like Jim."

"But I never thought he would turn out to be my father. Do I look like him?"

Mother took the plates off the table. "You look more like me, but you act like Jim."

"How?" Christine was eager to know.

"Determination," her mother said. "Your turn for the dishes."

It was early afternoon when Christine went back to Jim's. She knew the first question she was going to ask him: how did you find us. And that after so many years.

Jim was working in the garden when she arrived. "Weeds come uninvited," he said. "I don't want them to take over again. Not after the work I've done to get rid of them. Come inside." He leaned the hoe against the shed and opened the front door. He washed his hands in the kitchen sink. "Let's sit in the living room. You want anything? Juice, pop?"

THE OLD HOUSE

"No thanks. Just had lunch." Christine's butterflies appeared again in her stomach. What was he going to tell her? She saw her mother's letter on the table. Jim sat down in an armchair.

"Did your mom tell you anything about me and what I wrote?"

"Sort of. That you were badly injured in the war and that's why she didn't hear from you."

Jim nodded. "Yes, it took a long time for me to heal after the operations. And then I needed lots of therapy to get back on my feet. When I was strong enough I had to find work. But I never forgot your mother. You look a lot like her."

"Yeah, that's what she told me. But she said that I'm acting like you."

Jim smiled. "Did she? In what way? Not bad I hope."

"Mom only said 'determination.'"

"She is right about that." He picked up the letter. He was quiet for a few minutes. "You're too young to understand some of the things. I'm sorry we had to give you such a terrible shock in finding out that your dad wasn't your real father."

Christine rubbed her nose. "He was the only dad I knew, and he still is. I talk to him at night. Maybe he listens."

Jim nodded. "I said before you're a smart girl."

"Why didn't you marry someone else?"

Jim sat back. "Because of my injuries I wouldn't have been able to work like an ordinary husband and support a family. That wouldn't have been fair to my wife. Also your mother was still on my mind. Those are the reasons why it took me that long to get the courage to find you."

"How did you find us?" Christine was practically itching to find out.

"Long story. I'll make us some tea. You drink tea?"

Christine nodded. "Yeah, but not black. Ugh!"

Jim laughed and went into the kitchen. Christine didn't quite understand what his injuries had to do with working. He was working now in the garden and the house. That was hard to do. Maybe Mom knew more about this mystery. When Jim came back with two cups of tea Christine was more than ready to hear more of his story.

"When I couldn't find your mom in Vancouver, I searched for the girl friend she had at the time. I was lucky I found her. She told me that your mom had moved away years ago because she was pregnant and couldn't stay there. She gave me her last address in Penticton. When I got there I was told by her neighbors that she had married and moved to Peachland." Jim paused and drank some tea.

Christine couldn't help fidgeting. "And then?"

"I needed to know about the baby," Jim continued. "I was sure I was the father. By that time ten years had gone by. I checked the hospital records and the church for christening records. There it was: a girl, named Christine."

"Were you glad?" Christine asked. *He should've been.*

THE OLD HOUSE

"To tell you the truth, I felt guilty that I made your mom go through all those problems alone. As I said before, it took me some time to get up enough courage to come here. But I needed to find you and your mom and make sure you were okay."

"How did you find this old house?"

Jim put the teacup down. "Oh, just looking around. Again I was lucky. This house was exactly what I needed and it had been for sale for a long time. When you came by the first day, I knew you were my daughter."

Christine shook her head. "Weird. And you couldn't tell me?"

Jim shook his head. "That wouldn't have been very wise. I knew you had a good family. The last thing I wanted was to interfere. And your mother was happy. I saw her a few times at the market. But I made sure she didn't notice me. I didn't want to give her a shock."

Still another question. "Why did you leave and not tell me? I was very hurt."

"I developed problems and had to go back to the hospital. Also I needed some distance from your family. I wasn't sure I could stay here without you knowing who I was." Then he smiled. "I was glad to get your letter, even though it was sad that your dad died. I felt it was okay to come back now."

"Whew, good thing I did write," Christine said. "I just knew I had to find you and tell you. I wanted you to come back and we would be friends again. And the house needed you."

Jim nodded. "We will be friends, more than ever, now. Any more questions?"

"When will you and Mom get together?"

"I'll leave that up to your mother. I don't want her to be uneasy about the neighbors and the possibility of gossip. Also—" he stopped and took a breath. "Even now I'm not sure whether we should be together."

What now? Christine sat up. "Why not? You said you loved Mom."

"That's just it. Your mother is still young and I might not be the right husband for her."

"I don't understand." Why was Jim so serious now? Disappointment crept into Christine's stomach. "I'm sure Mom still loves you, too."

Jim looked at the letter on the table. "It all has to do with my war injuries. Maybe your mom can explain it better to you."

Christine felt panic rising up. "But I don't want you to leave again, ever."

"No, I won't, I promise. I'll look after you and your mother. I have a lot to make up for all those lost years. Give it time, Christine, and talk to your mom. She knows what I'm talking about." Jim got up. "I'm so happy we had this talk. I still love your mother, I always have. You can tell her that." He put out his hand. Christine got up, too, and

THE OLD HOUSE

grabbed it. "I'll never replace your dad, but I'll love you just the same."

On her way home, Christine fought conflicting emotions. Yes, Jim had answered the questions she'd asked. But if two people loved each other they should be together, shouldn't they? She had read stories about soldiers who had come home from the war with one arm or leg missing and they still got married. Why was this so different? Well, Mom would have to explain this. Maybe they could just be friends, very good friends, at least for now.

CHAPTER 11

During the next week the weather was rainy and stormy. One night the wind knocked out the power in most of the town. Tree branches were flying everywhere. Christine got soaked a few times walking home from school because one of her umbrellas flew away and the other one broke. What a spring, she thought. She pitied the poor flowers that had dared to bloom already.

During one dark evening when the power was out in the house, Christine found it a good time to ask her mother about the things that were on her mind. "What does Jim mean when he says he can't get together with you because of his injuries? What's the difference if he loves you?"

Mom didn't answer for a long time. She seemed to search for words. Then she looked at Christine over the candle they had lit. "Being married isn't just living together in the same house. It involves at lot of emotions and things people want from each other." She smoothed out the edge of the tablecloth. Then she continued. "Get the big doctor's book from the shelf. I'll show you."

Christine went into the living room and shone the flashlight into the bookshelf. There it was, a pretty heavy volume. She handed the book to her mother.

She leaved through a lot of pages. "Here it is. When Jim got hurt, his leg from the knee down got damaged so badly that it had to be amputated." Mom pointed to the man in the picture.

"How come he can walk?" Christine shuddered at the image of the injury.

"Didn't you notice that he has a slight limp?" Mother asked. "He had to get used to a prosthesis, a man-made leg."

"How does that work? What is it made of? Does it hurt? It must be so heavy." Christine wiggled her right leg. What could anyone do with only half a leg?

"It wasn't easy and it took a long time. At first it was made partly out of wood and iron. Then his leg got infected and he had to go back to the hospital. Now he has a new leg made out of lighter material, a certain kind of plastic."

Christine still couldn't understand. "So he is okay now. Why can't you get together? It's only his leg."

Mother shook her head. "No, that isn't all of it. All the terrible fighting and seeing so many people and his friends being killed during the war had made him so depressed that he couldn't cope with life. They call it being shell-shocked.

THE OLD HOUSE

Jim spent a few years in an institution. That is still very shameful for him, and it's better that nobody knows about it."

"You mean he was going crazy?" Christine couldn't even imagine that. Jim acted normal like everyone else.

"No, not that bad, just...some soldiers weren't able not get rid of the nightmares. Others shut out the real world. They all needed doctors to help them get back to normal, and that took time. Maybe he feels that he still has days where he is sad and can't work properly. I understand that, but Jim thinks that he can't support us like a normal husband. And I don't want him to feel uncomfortable or pressured."

"But—but—"

"Your dad hasn't even been gone a year," Mother interrupted. "Be patient."

"At least Jim promised that he wouldn't leave again. Do you still love him?"

Mother closed the book. "I can't answer that right now, Christine. I'm just glad he found us and that he is here. I never thought it would happen."

Christine still couldn't understand the part about Jim not able to work. He'd renovated the garden of the old house and was even working on the house itself. How much more able should a person be? Besides, she had always seen him cheerful and funny, never sad. But she knew badgering her mother more about meeting Jim would only result in her getting angry. Unless Christine could think of something way out of the ordinary, she would just have to wait.

ご〜〜

On the weekend, after the sky cleared, Christine and her mother cleaned up the yard. They heaped all the broken branches into one big pile. Mr. Whiting, who had taken care of the old house before, offered to load it on his old truck and cart it away. When Christine went by the old house later in the day, she could see smoke and flames from the yard. Jim had put a big pile of branches together and had made a bonfire.

"Hey," he called. "Want to roast marshmallows?"

"Marshmallows?" Christine thought that was funny. It reminded her of going camping and sitting around a campfire. Jim found some thin branches and brought out a bag of marshmallows.

"Might as well have fun," he said.

Christine looked at him and couldn't help wondering about the pain and disappointment Jim must have felt. How difficult it must have been to get used to walking on a wooden leg. She thought he must be the most courageous person in the world.

Later she told her mother about the marshmallows. Mother laughed. "That's Jim for you, always quirky and at his Jimmiest."

THE OLD HOUSE

83

ఴఴఴ

Not long after the stormy days, the weather turned warm and sunny. Gardens showed off their flowers and bushes in full bloom. It was hard for anyone to stay indoors. Christine and Ellie thought this was a perfect time for a bike ride along some back roads. The greening fields and the farmhouses with their barns in the sunshine looked like picture postcards. Cows and horses seemed to enjoy the outdoors and were munching on grass or peacefully wandering around.

On a small path between the trees Ellie took the lead. Christine was looking around, wondering whether she could see deer or rabbits when suddenly her bike shot out from under her. With a scream, she toppled sideways to the ground with the bike on top of her. She heard a crack and felt a sharp pain in her head. For a moment, everything went dark. Then she heard Ellie's voice.

"Christine, what happened? Can you get up? Come on, try." She grabbed the bike and, with a grunt, pulled it off Christine.

Christine winced as she shook her head. "I can't. My head hurts, I'm dizzy and my arm feels funny."

"Here, you banged you head on this rock. Try and move your head, I'll push it away." Ellie grabbed the stone wrested it to the side.

"What happened to my bike?" Christine groaned.

Leftover branches from the storm lay strewn on the path. One of them had flipped up and wedged itself through the spokes of her front wheel.

"Okay, you keep still. I'll get help. Don't move!" Ellie was already on her bike pedaling off.

Christine moaned. "Oow, my head. I can't move my arm either." She got mad at herself. "I just wasn't looking where I was going. Mom will be furious." She tried again to get up but everything kept spinning around and it made her sick. With another groan, she lay down again. Ellie was back soon.

"The farmer is calling the ambulance. You cracked your head, your brain got rattled."

All Christine wanted to do was close her eyes. "I just want to sleep, I'm tired."

"No, don't. Hear the sirens? Those people will help you." Ellie waved at the ambulance rumbling and inching its way along the path. It stopped and the paramedics came running with a stretcher.

One of them bent over Christine. "Hey, what happened? Where does it hurt?"

Christine told him about the rock and her arm. She cried out when he tried to move it. "Might be broken," he said. They lifted her onto the stretcher and turned to Ellie.

"Want to come along?"

"No, I'll follow you on my bike." She looked at Christine's bike and its crooked front wheel. "Christine, I'll

THE OLD HOUSE

85

ride by your house and tell your mom, okay? Then someone will have to pick up this wreck later."

"Okay," Christine mumbled.

The medic had secured her arm in a sling, but now it hurt more than her head. Bumping along the back road in the ambulance made the pain worse. She was glad when the ambulance finally reached the smooth surface of the paved street.

All the way to the hospital she scolded herself. *Why didn't I watch the ground? How could I have missed those branches? And my bike is broken, too. Stupid, stupid, stupid!*

CHAPTER 12

The doctor at the hospital confirmed that she had broken her arm. "I'll have to set it properly, so we'll put you to sleep for a while." He examined her head. "There is a good-sized lump."

"I might've rattled my brain," Christine said.

The doctor laughed. "Well, it's still in there, just shook up a bit. We'll keep an eye on it."

Christine got a bit anxious when a nurse wheeled her into the operating room. "Don't worry," she assured her. "When you wake up your mother will be here. And you'll have a cast on your arm, so everyone can write their names on it."

The doctor put a mask on her face and made her count backwards from ten to...

When Christine opened her eyes again she didn't know where she was. She saw the nurse's face close to hers.

"Time to wake up," she said.

It seemed to Christine that just a few minutes had passed. "I'm done already?"

"Yes, dear. How are you feeling?"

Christine didn't really know, only that her stomach felt queasy. "I hope I don't throw up."

"Take some deep breaths," the nurse said. "It's the anesthetic, it will get better. Does your arm hurt?"

Christine tried to move it but the cast held it stiff. "Don't know, I guess so."

The nurse laughed. "You'll have to put up with it for a few weeks. Here's your mom."

Mother came from behind the nurse. Her eyes were all anxious as she sat down on the bed. "What happened out there on the road? Ellie told me about the branch in your wheel."

"Yeah, I'm sorry I didn't pay attention to the road. Can the bike be fixed? Do I have to pay for it?"

Mother stroked Christine's forehead. "Never mind the bike. I'm just glad that you're okay. How is your head?"

Christine wriggled her neck. "Just a bit sore."

Mother stayed for a little while, and then she left to go back to work.

After she had gone Christine wondered what to do now. How long did she need to be there? she wondered. She looked around. There were three more empty beds in the room. It would have been nice to have another girl to

THE OLD HOUSE

talk to, she thought. But she still felt woozy and, after a while, fell asleep.

When she woke up again it was evening. The nurse wheeled a table with food into the room. "Do you feel like eating?"

Christine wrinkled her nose. "Depends. What is it?"

"Soup and Jell-O pudding. We don't want to overload your stomach," the nurse answered. "Let me put the pillow behind your back. Sit up carefully."

"Why aren't there any other patients here?" Christine asked.

"One girl left when you came in, broken foot. The other one had her tonsils out and left the day before."

"Too bad. It would have been nice to have company."

Christine thought her mother's soup tasted better than this kind but the Jell-O pudding was all right. She was glad that she hadn't broken her right arm. Eating with her left hand would have been even more awkward.

Mother came once more after supper and brought her pajamas. "I have to work tomorrow, too," she said. "I'll check on you in the evening. In the meantime be good and do what the doctor and nurse tell you." She gave her a kiss and left.

"Yeah, Mom." *What else can I do?* Would Jim find out that she had had an accident? Would he come and visit her? She sighed. What a ruined day.

The next afternoon Ellie came by. She brought a big card signed by the kids in her class and some chocolates. "I thought probably no one else would bring any," she said.

"Did you see Jim? Did you tell him about my accident?" Christine asked.

"Yup. I told him all about it. He was quite upset and brought your bike home. That truck of his sure is rickety." She giggled. "I bet he'll bring you flowers."

Christine found it very hard not to tell Ellie about Jim being her father. Then she had another thought. "You know that my mom never wanted to meet him. What if they both visit me at the same time? Then they'll have to meet."

Both girls thought that would be hilarious.

"Fat chance," Ellie said. "Don't know why your mom is so stubborn about it."

"You know something? We just have to make sure they come here at the same time."

Christine got excited about her idea. "My mom is coming tomorrow evening. Someone has to tell Jim to visit, too. Neither of them should know that the other one is here."

"In other words, you want me to help arrange this," Ellie said.

"Well, I'm stuck here but you can tell Jim to *please, come*, that I'm in a lot of pain."

THE OLD HOUSE   91

Ellie snorted. "Oh, boy, I'm sure he'll fall for that. Okay, I'll try to convince him. Can I have one of your chocolates?"

"Go ahead, open the box." That was Ellie for you, Christine thought.

Ellie signed her name on Christine's cast and, with a thumbs-up, went out the door.

This had to work, Christine thought, it was her only chance. At least something good would come out of her accident. The question was, how would Mother react? Well, it couldn't be any worse than it was now.

The doctor came by before supper.

"How is your head?" he asked.

"I still have a headache," Christine said. "But I want to get up. It's boring lying around."

The doctor felt her head. "Well, the lump is getting smaller. But if you feel dizzy, sit down, okay? I'll give you something for your headache."

When Christine got up and walked around a bit, she felt better. She was hoping to go home soon. The cast on her arm was cumbersome but she could manage and she would have her own things to spend her time with.

Her mother came again after supper.

"I miss you at home," she said. "It's too quiet and lonely."

"Is my bike a total wreck?" Christine asked. Her usual butterflies had been flitting around in her stomach again. *Will my plan work?*

"It's all fixed up," came a voice from the door.

Christine knew that voice. It was Jim. He gave her mother a surprised look. Christine saw her mom stiffen. It looked like she wanted to get up.

"Please, stay." Jim's eyes pleaded with her mother. "It's safe enough here, don't you think?"

Mom just looked at him with big eyes and sat down again.

"After all, I have to make sure my new daughter is all right. Here are some daffodils out of the garden." He pulled up a chair and sat down. "Besides, I have to sign your cast."

Christine took the flowers, and then looked from Jim to her mother. She started to giggle. "So, I had to fall off my bike for you two to meet? That's not fair."

Her mother shook her head and gave a quiet laugh. "You win. Both of you."

Jim laughed, too. "As I said before, you have a smart daughter—correction: *we* have a smart daughter."

Christine could have jumped for joy. So, her idea had worked: they had both come at the same time and Mom had not panicked. Ellie had done a good job. To keep Mom and Jim from just looking at each other, Christine gave a detailed account of her adventure with her fall, Ellie's rescue, and the ambulance ride. She was very surprised when, after a while, Mom and Jim got up together.

She heard Jim say, "Let's have some coffee in the cafeteria."

THE OLD HOUSE

She didn't hear if Mom agreed but she had the feeling that she, after all these years, couldn't say *no* any longer.

That evening, before going to sleep, Christine closed her eyes and envisioned her dad sitting by her bedside.

"I hope you can hear me, Dad. A lot has happened. I broke my arm and banged my head. It hurt but it's okay now. Remember Jim? You thought he was all right. Well, he and Mom have finally met." Christine laughed a little. "Ellie and I helped it along a bit. I hope you don't mind them being friends now? I still love you." She curled up under her blanket. A great ending to an unforeseen disaster.

Mother would probably wait until a year after Dad's death to invite Jim over. That was the rule and, after all, what would the neighbors say? Yeah, no matter what, they would have something to talk about anyway. Christine giggled to herself. If she had listened to Mother, Jim wouldn't be here now. She had done what she thought was the right thing to do. She had disobeyed her mom but this time it had been for the good of all of them. Maybe, after a while, they would be real family again.

She looked at her arm in the cast. Jim had written, *I am proud of you, love Jim* on it. What a strange way to bring them together after all these years. Absolutely perfect.

About the Author

Gisela Woldenga was born in Oldenburg, Germany, on July 21, 1934. As soon as she could read she started to write: little poems and fairy tales. She still has some of them. When she finished high school, she started working in a lawyer's office, mostly disputes over last wills and testaments and property. Then she moved on to the main taxation office. She met her husband through pen-paling—he was already in Canada—and she joined him in 1954 in Ontario. She had her first baby in 1956, her second one in 1957 then moved to Vancouver BC and added another baby in 1961.

Woldenga picked up music (piano) again in 1964, started teaching shortly after, and taught until about 6 years ago. In the meantime she wrote articles, poems, children's stories. She also took up acting after her kids were safely gone, in 1998. Lots of fun! She's still doing it whenever possible. After some courses in writing for children, she started publishing. From there on into short stories for adults and finally to books.

Made in the USA
Charleston, SC
01 December 2012